HIS BOUNTIFUL GIFTS

MEN OF THE SEA BOOK ONE

SADIE KING

HIS BOUNTIFUL GIFTS

A bad boy on the run washes up on my beach and claims me as his...

I found him on the sand, cut and lashed by the storm, his body naked and marked with ink that tells of a dark past.

Ronan needs a place to hide. My caravan becomes his safe haven—and I, his willing nurse.

Until his past tracks him down. And I must give up the one man who was my salvation.

His Bountiful Gifts is a forced-proximity instalove romance featuring an OTT obsessed man and the curvy woman he claims as his own.

PROLOGUE

I conjured him out of the ocean.

It was the night the storm hit Temptation Bay. Waves thrashed against the rocks. The sea was crying and moaning like she was in pain. Leaden clouds pressed so low in the sky I thought they would smother us all.

Rain pelted the trailer so hard I couldn't hear the incantations I chanted as I gripped Gram's tea-stained cards, their edges turned up from use.

I laid the cards that night, as I had every night since Gram left me. I called to her spirit, seeking comfort from another realm that I wasn't getting from this one.

With the storm raging around me, I lit Gram's candles, sprinkled herbs at the windows. I threw the dice, and I set the cards. I used everything Gram had taught me.

Remembering the ancient words, I chanted to the goddess of the oceans.

Gram would ask for guidance, but I asked for deliverance.

The ancient words whispered from my throat grew louder as the storm raged until I was shouting, worked into a frenzy with the howling wind.

A window shattered. The storm or a spirit, I couldn't be sure. The candles flickered and died. The cards blew off the table, and I fell exhausted onto the bed.

Of course, I didn't really believe Gram's cards, or chants, or the power of herbs to call the gods. It was comforting to believe in a spirit world, but I didn't think they could help me. It was just a diversion. A last-ditch hope before I accepted my fate.

I didn't think it would work…

1

ULA

The pre-dawn sky holds no trace of the oppressive clouds from yesterday as I step out of my car and head down the walkway to the beach. The sea simmers and swirls, bubbling around rock pools and tugging at the shore.

The day after a storm is always my favorite time to walk along the beach and watch the foamy waves tug at the debris tossed onto the shore, as if they have no memory of the raging sea and devastation from the night before.

I woke before dawn and drove the two miles to the beach, eager to see what gifts the storm has brought me.

Sails are broken at the marina, and roof panels have been blown off the small cluster of buildings along the Temptation Bay beachfront.

A cool breeze hits my neck, and I pull Gram's shawl tight around my shoulders. My bare feet sink into the ground, wet sand squelching between my toes as I start along the beach.

Driftwood, twisted and worn by the water, lies scattered across the sand as I pick my way along the shoreline.

There's a shape up ahead, perhaps a particularly large

piece of driftwood that the tide has thrown up onto the shore.

In the brightening dawn light, it appears more like an animal, maybe a seal that's swam too far south. Or a small whale separated from its pod and beached in the storm.

As I approach the object, the sun breaks the horizon, casting her first golden rays across the sand.

My breath hitches in my throat. It's not a seal. It's not a whale, and it's certainly not a piece of driftwood.

The storm has brought me a man.

Pale light creeps over the figure lying on his back on the sand. I take a few steps closer, peering curiously at him.

His shoulders are massive, the size of small boulders. Seaweed twists over taut muscles and dark ink patterns that snake down his arms, around his wide chest, and down to his…

Oh my. I take a step back.

He's naked.

My throat goes dry, and I swallow hard.

There's a naked man washed up on the beach. I should run back to my car and call for help. But my curiosity is too strong.

Stepping forward, I allow my gaze to sweep his torso, taking in the ink that swirls and twirls in patterns of hidden meaning under a layer of chest hair.

My gaze follows the thin line of hair from his chest over his hard belly. Even while lying still, the outline of his abs can be seen. My eyes continue down to the mound of thick, curly hair and what lies beyond.

His member hangs thick and dark, curled down the side of one thigh like a sleeping sea snake.

A gasp escapes my lips.

Because, yeah, it hangs halfway down his thighs now. What would this ocean giant look like hard? An image of his thick purple member—hard as rock and dripping juice—jumps into my head.

There's a stirring in my core and a tug so strong I stagger to my knees. Dampness floods my panties, and I have to catch my breath.

The ocean has certainly been bountiful with her gifts this morning.

I tear my gaze away from the man's bounty to study his face. Dark hair is plastered to his cheeks, and his eyes are closed. His lips are tinged blue.

Shit.

Here I am fantasizing about his giant squid when the man might not even be alive. Fear and a sense of loss flood me, which is stupid because I only found him a minute ago.

Reaching out to take his pulse, my fingers are about to press down on his throat when the man moves.

His hand shoots out of the sand and grasps my wrist, a movement so quick it makes me gasp.

My eyes flick to his face, and he's staring right at me, his eyes as blue and stormy as the ocean. The intensity of his look makes my pulse quicken and my core turn to liquid.

It feels like hours that his gaze is locked with mine, but it must only be a few seconds. Then his eyes move down my face to my mouth open with shock.

His look travels down my throat to my chest. I'm leaning over him, my top fallen open, and he must be able to see down my top.

He takes his time looking me over, and I feel myself melt under his gaze.

I catch movement out of the corner of my eye, and I glance down his body. Between his legs, the giant sea snake is stirring to life. I'm transfixed, terrified and turned on all at once.

It unfurls and hardens, the length stretching out down his

thigh. It's purple and thick and stirs feelings inside me I've never felt before. A need. A longing that none of the neighborhood boys have ever stirred in me.

I'm dripping wet, my breath coming in short, sharp pants. I let out a whimper.

The man groans, and my gaze darts back to his face. His eyes are dark and hooded. He croaks one word.

"Mine."

Then his eyes close, his grip on my wrist loosens, and he falls unconscious onto the sand.

2

RONAN

Sound comes to me in stilted waves. The crashing of the ocean against the shore. Seagulls cawing above me.

A warm sensation starts at my temples. Gentle fingers brush against my cold skin, the warmth of the touch sending waves of heat through my skull.

She's massaging my head. The angel who I glimpsed as if in a dream. She must be an angel, and I must be dead.

The last thing I remember is the creak of the boat as it broke apart, dashed upon the violent waves of the ocean, and grabbing for debris in the water as powerful waves crashed around me.

When I next opened my eyes, the angel knelt beside me, her sweet, innocent face graced with sweeping long eye lashes and plump cherub lips popped open in surprise.

She must be an angel, and I must be in heaven because I can hear her now, humming under her breath. No, not humming. Chanting. The words are foreign to me—I don't speak angelic—sweet and guttural as she runs her fingers over my temples.

If I've died and gone to heaven, then it's as good a place as everyone hopes it is. My eyes flicker open, and the angel is kneeling behind my head. Her soft fingers run over my skull, holding my head in her hands. It's a pleasant sensation that sends tingles through my broken body.

She's sitting up straight, her blonde hair falling over her shoulders. Then she leans forward. Her eyes are closed. The chanting gets stronger. Maybe this is some ritual to get me into heaven. Maybe she's pleading for my soul. Because, to be honest, I'm surprised I'm here. With the deeds I've done, I belong in the other place.

The angel leans forward, and her top slips open. Her breasts are pushed together, straining against her bra. It's what I saw when I first opened my eyes.

Those perfect breasts, big and heavy, hint at the curves of her body. The v of her cleavage makes me want to slide my tongue between the crevice, bite her delicate skin, and make her scream my name.

I'm definitely not getting into heaven if I'm having dirty thoughts about an angel.

Luckily, she's got her eyes closed when my dick stirs. As I watch her breasts sway back and forth, my cock hardens.

I've swallowed half the ocean; my chest feels like there's a boulder sitting on it, and there's a pain in my side that feels like a deep cut. But there's nothing wrong with my cock.

It aches to slide itself between those breasts, to claim this angel for what I know her to be.

Mine.

Her eyes flick open, and the chanting stops. She's leaning over me, looking down, and she glances at my hard cock swaying between my legs like a piece of driftwood.

"You're alive then."

She sits back on her haunches, and I can't see her

anymore. It's like the sun going out. I swivel my shoulders, needing to see my angel.

Pain shoots through my body, and I let out a guttural groan.

"Don't try to move." Her voice is as sweet as the heavens. "I'll call an ambulance."

"No."

I'm getting the feeling that I'm not dead and she's not an angel. Although to me she always will be.

"No ambulance."

Her warm fingers trace a line on my torso, and there's a delicious sensation marred by pain from some new wound there.

"You're bleeding." Her hands press firmly around the wound, making me wince.

"It doesn't look deep, but it needs treating."

With some effort, I pull myself onto my elbows to survey the damage. There's a gash on my side that's muddied with seaweed and sand.

"Looks okay to me."

She shuffles around to the side so she can see me better, and I get a good look at her angel face. She looks concerned. "You need fixing up. Is there someone I can call?"

She's not pressing the ambulance, which is a relief. Maybe whatever small coastal town I've washed up in has the same distrust of the authorities that I do.

"There's no one."

I pull myself up to a sitting position and check out my surroundings.

I've washed up in a small bay with cliffs at one end and a marina at the other.

There's a line of buildings near the marina that look damaged from the storm. It won't be long before there's people milling about, come to assess the damage.

I need to get away from here. Fast.

My angel's watching me. She seems calm, not at all scared by my naked, tattooed body and hard cock, which I can't seem to get under control.

"Does it always do that?" she asks, nodding to the aching appendage between my legs.

"Only when I see something I want."

"Oh."

Her mouth pops open, and I stifle a groan. Those lips wrapped around my cock would be exquisite, but there'll be plenty of time for that. Now that I've found my angel, I won't let her go.

I've learned to trust my instincts about people, to trust my gut. And my gut is telling me this innocent angel could be my salvation.

My dick's telling me that too, but he can't always be trusted.

"No ambulance, no cops. I need somewhere to go, somewhere quiet."

She meets my gaze, and there's understanding there. She nods slowly.

"Come with me."

Wincing, I pull myself off the sand. My legs are numb, and I stumble a few times. The angel offers her arm and I lean on her. We must look ridiculous. I'm a good few heads taller than her and butt naked.

"What's your name, angel?"

"Ula."

"I'm Ronan."

She half turns to me, and her lips curl into a smile. "Like a seal."

She must see the confusion on my face. "In my Gram's old tongue, Ronan means seal. I knew you were a gift from the ocean."

I don't know what the fuck she's talking about, but I like the way she smiles at me. She thinks I'm the gift, but I already know she's my angel, my salvation. And she's mine.

3

ULA

The last of the sunrise is fading into day when I park my car down the road from the trailer park. Aside from Meredith, who's up tending to her squalling baby, there's no sign of the other residents.

Gram's caravan, or mine now, is at the far end of the park. It's the shabby two-bedroom adorned with lucky charms and a string of garlic hanging off the awnings to ward off bad spirits. Her well-stocked herb garden borders the sides in neat planters.

"Keep to the shadows if you don't want to be seen and follow me."

Ronan's body has been weakened by the ocean, but he doesn't make a sound, though I can see his side causes him pain.

We reach the caravan, and I glance around before opening the door and letting him in. No one sees us. It's too early for most of the residents here.

Ronan is a giant in the small trailer. He towers over me, his head nearly scrapping the ceiling. Scattered on the table are the tarot cards and burned down candles, evidence of my session from last night.

The broken windowpane has been stuffed with a blanket, and glass adorns the floor.

"Storm damage," I say quickly.

Ronan has Gram's shawl wrapped around his body but he's shaking violently, his lips a pale blue.

His body was battered by the ocean, he's been cut, and he might have hypothermia. If he doesn't want medical assistance, then it's up to me and Gram's herb garden to get him fixed up.

"You need a hot shower and dry clothes."

He doesn't protest as I hand him a towel and show him the small shower room.

While he warms up, I rifle through my drawers in search of something for him to wear. There's an old checkered shirt he might fit and Gram's jogging bottoms.

I lay them out on the bed and step out to the herb garden.

Gram taught me all of the healing herbs, and I pick a bunch of echinacea and lemon balm, which should help the pain and work as an antiseptic.

"You left your water running."

I startle at the sound of the voice, dropping my scissors into the dirt.

Jeremy crouches to pick them up, his hand "accidentally" brushing against my knee.

"I can get them," I say quickly, plucking the scissors out of the soil.

Jeremy gives me what I guess is supposed to be a smile, but on his pinched face, it looks more like a grimace.

"Big storm we had last night. I was going to come and check you were okay."

"I'm fine. I don't mind a storm."

I stand up and back away toward the door of the trailer. If

Ronan decides to get out of the shower now, Jeremy will wonder who turned the water off.

"Want to head to the beach and see the damage?"

His eager eyes flick down my body and land on my breasts. It's where they stay for the rest of the conversation.

"No thanks. Got stuff to do."

Jeremy licks his lips. "You want to come and hang out later? My dad's gonna be out."

And that's what passes for seduction in Temptation Bay.

It's the kind of proposition I've gotten ever since my tits grew and boys started noticing me. Jeremy's not a bad kid. He's just like any other boy who's grown up around here. Dull and horny.

He's what Grant was like before he knocked up Meredith, and now they're in a trailer of their own with a screaming baby to look after.

It's what's expected of me growing up around here, especially now that Gram's passed. Choose a local boy and start a family.

I've resisted all of the advances so far. But my options are running out. One of these days, I'll be forced to accept a boy like Jeremy, and next thing I know, I'll have a squalling baby of my own and a husband who drinks too much.

Which is why I was calling the spirits last night, appealing to the storm for a way out. And it looks like my pleas were answered.

4

RONAN

Ula's towel is like a dish cloth on me, hardly covering my nakedness. I pull it around my waist as best I can and step out of the shower.

Ula's standing over a pot in the kitchen and looks up at me as I pry open the shower door. I'm feeling lightheaded, probably from swallowing too much sea water, but the smile she gives me is like a tonic to my soul.

"There's some clothes in the room at the end."

Ula indicates one of the doors, and I head for it. Before I can get all the way, the room tilts sideways, and my legs give out.

I catch myself on the wall, propping myself up with my shoulder. Ula's soft hand comes up to my forehead, and the cool of her hands against my hot skin is a salve.

"You're burning up."

I hate this feeling. Weakness.

"I'm fine." I try to stand up, but my damn legs have other ideas. "I just need to rest for a moment."

She gives me a scolding look. "You need to get to bed. You've got a fever."

Her hands go to her hips and her forehead creases. She's bossing me around and it's fucking adorable. I've got a fever, all right. A fever for her.

"All right, angel. Show me the bed."

Ula's hands are surprisingly firm as she guides me to the door at the end of the caravan. The blinds are drawn, and it has a musty smell, like it hasn't been lived in for a while. A peach-colored comforter with a frilly trim sits neatly over a double bed.

"This was Gram's room." There's a tremor in her voice.

"Ah shit, I'm sorry, angel."

If her Gram's just passed away, then Ula's all on her own. All the more reason she needs me. Except right now, the world is going blurry, and it feels like there's a furnace inside my body. I'm the one who needs her.

"I'm making you a tincture for infection, and I'll get willow bark for the fever."

She bustles out of the room, and I hear the banging of pots coming from the small kitchen.

As the fever takes me, I lie on the bed with my body burning up. Ula returns and lifts my head, making me drink a foul-tasting liquid, then gets to work dressing my wound.

Her nimble fingers wash out the wound, and she douses it with ointment. I bite the side of my mouth as she threads a needle through my skin, stitching the flesh back together.

Her drink has made me sleepy and the room blur.

Before I pass out, I grip her wrist, and she looks up at me startled.

"No one must know I'm here, angel."

"Shhhh." She puts her finger to her lips. "Rest."

Her deep-green eyes are the last thing I see before I let the fever take me.

5

ULA

My phone lights up with an incoming message and my first instinct is to ignore it. But it's probably Mira, again, wondering why she hasn't seen me along the waterfront.

I send a quick reply telling her I'm still not feeling well. Guilt gnaws at me as I hit send. I don't like lying to my friends and if I don't put in an appearance soon she'll probably come up here to check on me. She probably would have already if her horrid uncle wasn't working her so hard in his cafe.

It's probably him that put her up to messaging me every day. I sometimes set up a fortune telling stall outside their cafe for the tourists that come to Temptation Bay and it's good for business.

I turn my phone to silent and leave it in the kitchen area before heading to Gram's room to check on Ronan.

It's been five days since Ronan washed up on the shore. Five days of caring for him, talking to him, sharing his space. Five days to fall in love with him.

Because, yeah, I think I love the solid man with the broken body.

The first few days he was here, he slept restlessly as he fought off the fever. I gave him drafts to help ease the pain and fed him Gram's chicken soup recipe with plenty of healing herbs.

As the fever broke, he became more cognizant, more aware of me. His gaze follows me around the room in a way that sets my entire body on fire.

Ronan doesn't talk much, and I don't ask questions.

I know he's hiding from something, but I don't want to know what it is. If he talks about it, he might make plans to leave. And I don't want him to leave.

For the first time since Gram left, I have a purpose. A man to care for. The only man I've ever met who I want to care for, whose eyes I don't mind following me around.

It only takes one swish of my hips and the bedsheets twitch, his sea snake coming to life.

I pretend not to notice, but my body grows hot, his gaze like scorching flames across my skin. My knees tremble and heat pools in my belly, my core tugging with a need only he will be able to satisfy.

At night, I touch myself, knowing Ronan's in the next room.

Now that he's stronger, his looks have become more demanding, more penetrating. They make my panties damp every time I feel his eyes on me.

I long for him to touch me, and I don't know what he's waiting for. But the more he waits, the deeper my ache. It deepens until my entire body is a ball of nerves, ready to come apart as soon as he rests his stormy eyes on me.

I'm rubbing the antiseptic salve on his cut, and every press of my fingers against his skin sets a fire under my fingertips as I smooth the lotion slowly over his wound and around the red skin surrounding it.

He takes a sharp intake of breath.

"Sorry." I pull my fingers back.

"You didn't hurt me."

He turns his head, and his eyes are hooded and intense as they rake over my body. My nipples pucker under his gaze, and there's a gush of wetness between my legs.

The room's suddenly too hot, and I need some air. While I long for him to touch me, I'm terrified of the intensity of my feelings, how easily I'll come undone by him.

"I need more rosemary."

In my haste to get out the door, I knock against my jar of salve, sending it spinning onto the floor. I pick it up quickly and stumble out of the room.

Throwing open the caravan door, I breathe in big gasps of air.

My body's on fire and I can't think straight. No one has ever made me feel the way Ronan does. It's like my body is out of control just from the way he looks at me.

My back presses against the cool wall of the trailer and I close my eyes, sucking in deep breaths.

Suddenly, a greasy hand touches my face. My eyes fly open. Jeremy's standing in front of me, his hand grazing my cheek.

"Don't touch me." I slap his hand away, and he takes a step back, offended.

"Didn't mean to scare you. Christ, it's only me."

His eyes rove over my breasts and heaving chest. "You look good today, Ula."

I can't hide my disgust. "Go away, Jeremy."

He takes a step closer, ignoring my protest. His hands come up to either side of my head, trapping me between him and the trailer

"You should start being nicer to me."

His eyes flick to my lips and his tongue darts out, like he's going to kiss me.

"Let me go." I struggle against him, but he's got me trapped against the caravan.

"Stop fighting me, Ula. You know we're gonna end up together. What other options do you have?"

"I don't need any other options." I push forward, trying to get away from him, but his arms are too strong.

"Who you think has been paying your rent since your Gram passed?"

The words make me stop cold. I thought Gram was all paid up for the year.

"That's right. You owe me, Ula."

Jeremy smiles thinly as my realization sets in. He's been paying my rent, paying for me to keep living here.

"Don't worry. I'm not gonna take you by force. I'm not an animal." His eyes flick over my body in a hungry look that makes my blood run cold. "But the sooner you realize we're meant to be together, the better."

"She said no."

The gravelly voice comes from the open door of the caravan. Jeremy takes a step back, the shock apparent on his face.

Even in Gram's too tight sweatpants, Ronan makes an impressive figure. He's not wearing a top, and his muscles ripple under the ink of his tattoos. With such a hard expression on his face, he looks like a messenger from the gods.

"Who the fuck are you?" Jeremy splutters.

"I'm Ula's other option. And if you're not gone in five seconds, I'll break your fucking nose."

Ronan takes a slow step down from the trailer.

"One…"

Jeremy's eyes narrow as he takes him in. His eyes scan over Ronan's tattoos, and his hands go up as he backs away.

"All right, man…"

"Two."

"I dig it…"

"Three." Ronan takes another step forward. This time, Jeremy turns and flees.

I've been watching with my jaw open. Ronan has been hiding in my caravan all week, and now he's just exposed himself to Jeremy and whatever other nosy neighbors are watching.

"What are you doing?"

Ronan closes the distance between us. His hand slides around my waist to pull me toward him.

"I'm showing the world who you belong to."

6

RONAN

"**B**ut people will see you?"

Ula's concern is fucking adorable. I brush her cheek with my thumb, wanting to brush away her worry lines.

"I don't give a fuck."

Her mouth pops open, making my dick instantly hard. "The world needs to see that you belong to me."

"But how about the people you're hiding from?"

"Let them come. This is more important."

Ula's staring at me in disbelief.

I haven't told her how I feel about her until now. It's time she knew. With a quick movement that pulls at my stitches, I lift her up and hoist her over my shoulder—'cause, yeah, I'm a fucking caveman where Ula's concerned.

She gives a surprised squeal as I carry her into the caravan.

I've waited long enough. I've watched my angel with my cock painfully hard. I would have waited until my body was fully recovered and able to give her the fucking she deserves, but with horny boys sniffing around, I have to claim her now.

My foot kicks the door shut and I slide her off my shoulder, her body pressing against mine on the way down.

So soft. So warm.

She's looking up at me wide-eyed and innocent as I run a hand over her cheek, down her throat, and over her delicious tits. Her lips part, and she shudders under my touch.

"Angel…"

My hands slide under her top and pull it over her head. Her white lacy bra holds her perfect tits, and I run my hand over them.

"My soul has been yours since I washed up on your beach." My lips move down her throat and whisper into her ear. "Now I'm going to claim your body as mine."

As I say the words, I yank at her bra, pulling it apart. She gasps in surprise as the fabric rips and her breasts fall out into my waiting hand.

I drop to my knees and take her left nipple into my mouth, sucking until it hardens under my tongue. She tastes like rosemary and lemons and everything fucking delicious.

Her hands run through my hair, pulling me toward her. She moans as I suck on her nipples, my greedy mouth wanting all of her.

Running my hand up her thighs, I stroke her damp panties, pulling a whimper from her. With a hard tug, I pull those panties right off. The sound of tearing fabric makes my cock ache. Her musky scent fills my nostrils. I need to taste her.

"Sit on the table for me, angel."

I prop her up on the table and spread her legs.

"Shouldn't we pull the curtain?" She glances through the open curtains at the trailer park.

"No." I shake my head. "I want everyone to see that you are mine."

As I say the words, I jam my finger into her wet cunt.

She gasps, her eyes go wide, and her mouth drops open. Sweet Jesus, I'm about to lose it and I'm not even in her pussy yet.

"I want everyone to see you being claimed."

My thumb rubs her hard nub as I say it and she whimpers. Her hands grasp the side of the table, and she leans back, opening herself to me.

It's a beautiful fucking sight. I slide another finger in, but her pussy's so tight I can barely get it in.

"You ever done this before, angel?"

She shakes her head. "No. I'm a virgin."

The words make my balls pull up tight.

"Say it again."

"I'm a virgin." She's breathless and needy and I want to be in her cunt so bad.

Dipping my head, I dive under her skirt. The musky scent is so strong I have to grip her thighs—or else I'll lose it.

Her animal scent brings out the animal in me. My mouth closes on her pussy, and I lick her juices until they're all over my face.

My fingers pump her while my tongue flicks her nub.

With my other hand, I pull my throbbing cock out of my pants. Pre-cum drips off the end. I take it in my fist, giving myself a slow, hard tug as I devour her sweet cunt.

Then she cries out, and I know she's over the edge. Her body trembles and her cunt squirts cream into my mouth. It's the sweetest nectar I've ever tasted.

I come out from under her skirt, and she's trembling and sweaty, her nipples perky and hard.

"Now I'm going to take that sweet cherry of yours."

She nods, which is all I need her to do. I tug her skirt off and flip her around so she's bent over the table.

Her pink asshole puckers as I rub my cock over it. She moans and pushes back into me as I reach around until I find her slippery folds.

My tip slides over her entrance, and it's like a fire inside my cock. I need to be inside her now.

"Hold onto the table, angel"

My dick pushes into her.

She gasps. "You're too big."

"You'll get used to it. Relax and let Daddy take care of you."

She goes limp against the table, and I slide myself in a little more.

"Ronan," she whines. "I don't think I can take you."

"Hush, sweetheart." I lean forward and brush her hair off her back, giving her some tenderness. "You were made to take me."

She cries out as I slide in a bit more. Her pussy's gripping me like a vise, and I think I might break her apart.

"Ronan," she cries. "You're too big."

Her words are working me into a frenzy. I'm trying to go slow for her, but all I want to do is slam in and destroy her pussy.

"Be still for Daddy, and let me take that cherry of yours."

She gasps and her pussy slickens, releasing its tight grip and letting me know my angel likes the dirty talk.

"I can't fit you," she pants, yet as she says each word, her hips slide toward me, sinking my cock deeper and deeper, making me groan like an animal.

"Fuuuck, Ronan. It feels good."

"That's right, angel."

Her pussy relaxes, and just as she sighs in relief, I slam forward, burying myself deep in her cunt. She screams and bucks, and I grab hold of her hips to keep my cock deep inside her.

"Ronan," she cries out. "Fuuuck."

I grab her hair and pull her head back until my mouth is near her ear. "You like that, little girl?"

"Fuck yes." My mouth closes over her throat, nipping and biting and leaving my mark on her.

"You're mine now, Ula. I claim you."

I release her hair and she falls forward, panting on the table.

"Fuck, Ronan. I didn't know it would feel like this."

"This pussy belongs to me, you understand?"

"Yes," she whimpers.

"No one else will touch this." With every word, I slam into her, fucking her hard. I want to leave her raw. I want to destroy her.

The caravan shakes as I slam into her. Ula looks back at me, wide-eyed

"Someone will hear us."

"I want them to hear us. I want everyone to know you are mine."

She grips the table and I stand up straight, pulling her hips back toward me. Her pink asshole winks at me, and I rub my thumb over the puckered hole.

"Ronan," she gasps.

My finger grazes her asshole. She cries out.

"Say my name, Ula."

I slam into her, and she pants. "Ronan."

"Say it louder. Every time I fuck you."

"Ronan."

"Scream it, angel. Who's the daddy who's fucking you?"

"Ronan!"

"That's it, angel. Who does your pussy belong to?"

"Ronan," she cries.

"Fuuuck."

My thumb works her pink hole while my dick slams into her pussy.

She's calling out my name, and I don't care if the whole trailer park hears. I want them to know I own this pussy. This pussy is mine.

My hands run down her tits, and her breathing gets shallower.

"I think I'm gonna come," she cries.

"Come for me, baby. I want to hear my name on your lips as you come.

She's screaming now. She's screaming my name over and over as I slam into her tight cunt, her pussy sucking the life out of me. I wait for her to fall over the edge before I let myself come.

It's a tidal wave of release, my cum spiraling out in ropes and coating her womb, marking her with my seed, breeding her. Making her mine.

She cries my name one more time before collapsing onto the table, panting.

I withdraw from her warm nest and bundle her into my arms.

"You're mine now, Ula. Whatever happens, you're mine."

I carry her into the bedroom and lay her gently down on the bed. Tucking her tired body between the sheets, I nestle behind her, my body fitting perfectly against hers. My angel. Destroyed and claimed.

7

ULA

My pussy hurts. My thighs are scraped raw. There's a sting from the bite marks on my neck and a large, stupid grin on my face.

My heart swells every time I think about the last few days with Ronan.

The things he's doing to me are filthy, delicious. My body's in a permanent state of arousal whenever he's nearby. And being holed up in a small caravan together means he's always nearby.

I'm humming to myself as I sprinkle fresh sage into the broth I've got brewing.

The hairs on the back of my neck stand on end, and I know without turning around that Ronan's behind me.

His hand slides around my waist and I lean against him, resting my head against his solid torso.

"Smells good."

He kisses my neck as he says it, and I'm not sure if he means the broth or me. His hand wanders to my breast, making my nipples pucker, and I feel his hardness pressing into my back.

I guess it's me that he likes the smell of.

Even though my pussy is raw from overuse, I'm wet down there as soon as he touches me. I push my hips against him and am satisfied to hear him groan.

"What are you doing to me, angel…"

His hand wraps around my throat, pulling my head back to kiss my scorching flesh.

"You've enchanted me with your spells…"

My body writhes against him as his warm breath moves down my throat, kissing the love bites, the marks he's left on me.

But is there truth in his words? I always thought Gram's spells and chants were superstitions, her card readings a way for an old woman to make a bit of pocket money from troubled neighbors in need of advice.

I never thought they would actually work. Despite the happiness I've felt over the last few days, there's also a feeling of foreboding deep in my stomach.

What if I really did conjure Ronan and he's under some kind of spell? When the spell breaks, he'll see me for the chubby, plain trailer park girl that I am.

When the spell breaks, he'll leave me.

The thought of Ronan leaving makes me shudder. I turn to face him. My arms go around his neck, clinging to him. His eyes meet mine, and he must see something of my fear in them.

"What's the matter, angel?"

His thumb rubs under my chin. It's such an intimate gesture. I've only known this man for a little over a week, yet I feel like I know him on a deeper level.

"I think I love you."

The words slip out unbidden, and I regret them immediately. Ronan stares at me for a moment, his expression unreadable. He opens his mouth to speak, then his eyes shift quickly to something out the window.

"Shit."

His grip on me loosens, and I turn to see what's got his attention.

There's a man striding through the middle of the trailer park. He's wearing the distinctive jacket of the Underground Crows, the motorcycle club that operates down the Sunset Coast.

The man nods at someone, and Jeremy comes slinking out of the shadows. They converse, as if they've spoken before. Then Jeremy lifts his hand and points toward my caravan.

"They've found me."

When I turn to Ronan, his expression is hard, and a bolt of fear goes through my belly. Whatever he was hiding from has caught up with him.

I want to tell him to hide, to run. But we're in a trailer. There's nowhere to go.

To my surprise, Ronan throws open the door.

The biker's head snaps up, and his eyes meet Ronan's.

My heart's in my mouth. I'm not sure what's going to happen as these two giant men stare each other down.

Ronan moves first. He steps out of the caravan slowly. The biker steps forward to meet him.

They eye each other warily.

Then they throw open their arms and embrace.

8

RONAN

It was only a matter of time before Jesse or one of the boys tracked me down. I sealed my fate when I let my urge to claim my angel overtake me.

I knew word would get out that I was here and someone would find me. I'm just glad it was my brothers—the Crows —who did.

"We thought you were dead." Jesse breaks from the hug and steps back, his arms still on my shoulders.

"I'm very much alive." The most alive I've ever felt in my fucking life.

His bright eyes give me a once over. "You been holed up here?" He scans the trailer park filled with rusty caravans with grass growing up around their wheels. "What you been doing for the last week?"

"I've been occupied."

He glances over my shoulder, and a knowing smile spreads on his lips. "I can see that."

I follow his gaze to Ula, who's standing in the doorway with her arms crossed, watching us closely. She looks so vulnerable standing like that, her soft body hunching in on itself, biting her nails nervously.

Her confession took me by surprise, and I didn't get a chance to respond. Now Jesse's here slapping me on the back.

"You got somewhere private we can talk?"

Ula steps out of the doorframe, and as I lead Jesse into the caravan, I see him take in the bite marks on her neck.

Good. He needs to know she's mine as well. The whole goddam world needs to know.

"I'll give you guys some privacy."

There's something off in Ula's tone, but before I can say anything, she slips out the door, shutting it behind her.

Jesse sits at the little table, and I squeeze in opposite him. With both of us in the caravan, it feels extra small.

"We thought you were dead," Jesse says again. "That storm..."

He shakes his head slowly. "How did you survive?"

I'm still not sure myself. I thought I was dead. I thought I had drowned, but I see now that some impossible force brought me here, brought me to Ula. But I don't tell Jesse that.

"Dunno, man. I washed up on the beach."

"Anyone see you?" He rubs his beard slowly, and I know what he really means. Do the Chaos Riders know I'm alive?

"Only Ula. She found me at sunrise, and I've been hiding here ever since."

Jesse nods slowly. "But the locals know you're here now."

He tells me about the kid who came to the clubhouse thinking he had some big news about a man hiding in the trailer park.

It must be Jeremy, the horny kid with the hots for Ula. He thought I was hiding from the Crows. He didn't realize I was a brother.

"You know you can't stay here, right?"

Jesse says it gently, as gently as a six-foot-something man with tattooed arms wearing a gang patch can. But he's right.

I did something bad. I sought retribution with the Chaos Riders, our rival gang, for something they did a long time ago that I just found out about. Something personal.

I bumped off one of their members, and I did it without the Crows' blessing.

"Bruno is out of prison soon." Jesse says. "He'll be looking for revenge on the Chaos Riders and he doesn't want anything blowing up before then."

Typical of Bruno our club President to still give orders from inside a jail cell. But I respect him and the patch too much to cause anymore trouble.

If I go back, it'll start a gang war. And no one wants that. The best thing for me to do is to disappear, which is what I was trying to do when the storm disrupted my plans.

I glance out the window.

Ula's tending to her herb garden, plucking weeds out of the soil. There's a slight crease on her brow, and I long to smooth it over and tell her everything's going to be all right. If only that were true.

"Yeah, I know."

Jesse follows my gaze. "I mean, really disappear, man. You need to leave the coast, leave the country. Or this whole thing is gonna blow up."

I wrench my gaze away from Ula.

"I'll be gone tonight."

Jesse smiles. "I'll miss you, brother, but I'm fucking glad you're not dead."

9

ULA

My fingers pluck at weeds in the garden, ripping them out by the roots.

I knew it couldn't last. Whatever wind blew Ronan to me has come to claim him. To take him away.

The spell is broken, and no matter what I do, he'll leave.

I don't notice the tears on my face until a drop falls on my hands. Swiping at my eyes, I stand up from the garden.

Jeremy is crouched on the stoop of his caravan, watching me, and he gives me a pitiful smile.

"I'm sorry, Ula."

"No, you're not."

He stands up and saunters over to me. "It's for the best. You don't want to get involved with a man like that."

There's no meanness in his tone, just concern. "I don't mind that you've been with him, Ula. I'll still take care of you."

Through my tears, it's like I'm seeing Jeremy for the first time. He's not just trying to get into my pants. I think he genuinely cares for me.

Maybe that's not so bad.

What I had with Ronan was too wild, too unpredictable. Maybe being with someone who loves you even if you don't love them back is not so bad. Plenty of people live their lives like that.

"I've got a construction job on the new development. I'm not a deadbeat. I can provide for a family, Ula."

Jeremy seems earnest, and perhaps that's all a girl like me can hope for. A man with a steady job who is fond of her.

Only now I know there's another way to feel. Now I know how my body and soul can be awakened. If I can't have that feeling, I'd rather be on my own.

"I need some time."

I pull away from Jeremy and walk along the path to the end of the trailer park. There's a picnic bench that looks out over a field of tall grass, and I sit there, staring at the grass blowing in the wind and thinking about nothing.

I don't turn around when I head the footsteps. I know it's Ronan, and I know what he's going to say. "You've come to say goodbye."

He sits next to me, and I steal a glance. His stormy eyes are deeper, more sorrowful. "I hope it's not goodbye."

If this is some farewell-but-not-goodbye speech, then it's not making me feel any better. Tears threaten my eyes, and I swipe at them with the back of my sleeve.

"I can't stay here, Ula."

Oh God. My chest constricts, and there's a pain in my heart that makes me want to double over. But I won't show him that. With all of my willpower, I remain sitting upright, even as my heart shatters.

"When will you go?" My voice comes out flat but steady.

"It has to be tonight. There's a boat I can take."

So, this is it. We don't even get a night together. No more falling asleep tucked snugly into his body. No more waking up with his arm draped over me. No more feeling alive and wanted and content.

His hand clasps mine, and I pull away.

"Ula…" His tone sounds hurt, but I refuse to look at him. I keep staring out at the grass. "Come with me."

The words take a moment to register. I glance at him, confusion written all over my face.

"Since I opened my eyes and saw you, angel, I knew you were mine. I thought I was dead when I washed up on that beach, but you brought me back to life."

He runs a hand over his hair and breathes out slowly. "This may sound stupid, but I have this feeling like I was called to you. Like we were meant to find each other."

I stare at him, wide-eyed. This doesn't sound stupid at all. The sea brought him to me, but maybe he also brought me to the sea. Maybe he's the reason I was down on the beach so early after the storm. Fate called to me, and I answered.

My chest lightens. My heart soars. Can Ronan really feel the same way about me as I do about him? We are meant to be together. The forces of fate threw us together.

He takes my hands in his. "I can't promise you an easy life, or an honest one. But I will love you fiercely and protect you for the rest of my days."

I'm too stunned to speak, and now the tears come in great, happy rivulets, streaming down my cheeks.

Ronan kisses the salty tears away. "What do you say? Will you disappear with me?"

My mind runs over my life at Temptation Bay. Since Gram passed on there isn't much left for me here, a caravan I owe debt on and a few friends that are moving on with their own lives.

I think of Mira at the cafe and the way her uncle mistreats her. But she has someone watching over her now although she's not aware of him yet. Mira will be just fine without me. "Yes, Ronan. Take me with you."

His mouth closes over mine, and this kiss is different. It's gentle, loving, and full of all the promises he just made.

My entire body springs to life. I conjured him out of the ocean, and together we'll return, letting the winds and sea goddesses guide us on our life's adventure.

EPILOGUE

ULA

Six years later…

Water laps at my feet as the sun breaks over the horizon. Behind me on the beach, the kids are sleeping in the hut we've called home for the last few weeks.

Last night I read the cards, and it's time to move on. It's time to continue on our path down the coast to the next town that calls to us.

The hairs on the back of my neck stand up, and I know without turning that Ronan is behind me.

"You're up early." His arms slide around my waist, and his warm breath nips at my neck. At his touch, there's a familiar tug in my core, and I let out a moan that's carried on the early morning tide.

"It's time to go." Ronan is used to my readings by now, the chanting and the calling.

It started as a way to remember Gram, but I've seen too many coincidences in this life not to believe there's something out there guiding us.

"Okay." Ronan accepts this without question, and I know

in a few hours we'll have the family packed up and on the road. But for now, we have the sunrise to ourselves.

Gram's old shawl is wrapped around my shoulders, and Ronan peels it off, letting it fall to the ground.

"Get on your knees." His gruff voice sends a shiver through me, and I sink to the ground. His rough hands are all over my body, pulling my night dress up and my panties off.

Ronan has a voracious appetite, and I'm happy to oblige.

He's already panting as he kneels behind me, grabbing my ass and lining his dick up with my entrance.

The cool pre-dawn air ripples along my bare buttocks, adding to the sensations humming through my body.

With a sharp thrust, he's inside me, and I let out a moan that's carried away on the ocean breeze.

His dick fills me up, awakening my nerve endings and turning my insides to liquid. Sharp sand grazes my knees as he pushes me down onto my elbows.

There may be fishermen out early or women hurrying to work, but that only makes me wetter. Someone might see my man claiming what's his. And I am all his.

Teeth nibble at my neck, and I cry out as the pressure builds in my belly.

"Fuuuck, Ronan. I'm going to come."

He grunts in response, and I know what he wants. What he needs to hear.

"Ronan!" I call, not caring who hears us.

I feel his cock lengthen, and that's enough for me. I'm over the edge, screaming his name.

I call his name over and over, howling it to the ocean, to the waves, to anything that can hear us. Letting everyone in this realm and the next know that I am his, that we belong together, and that what the gods threw together can never be torn apart.

He shoots his seed into me, grunting my name to the universe until we're both spent.

We lie together on the beach, watching the waves crash on the shore.

The gods sent us to each other, and we let them know with our lovemaking how much we value their gift.

THE BIKER'S REVENGE
UNDERGROUND CROWS MC

She's my enemy's daughter and my new obsession.

After three years inside, there's only one thing I want: revenge.
But when a retaliation goes wrong, I find myself with a fire cat captive—Scarlett, my enemy's daughter.
She's half my age and dripping with innocence. Scarlett becomes my revenge, and it's never been sweeter. But when her father comes for her, there's no way I'm giving her up.

The Biker's Revenge is a forbidden love, age-gap romance that starts with a kidnapping and ends with a happily ever after. Featuring an OTT obsessed hero and the curvy girl he claims as his own.

GET YOUR FREE BOOK

Sign up to the Sadie King mailing list for a FREE book!

You'll be the first to hear about new releases, exclusive offers, bonus content and all my news. You can even email me back. I love chatting with my readers!

To claim your free book visit:
www.authorsadieking.com/free

BOOKS BY SADIE KING

Sunset Coast

Underground Crows MC

Sunset Security

Men of the Sea

Filthy Rich Love

The Cod Cove Trilogy

Wild Heart Mountain

Military Heroes

Mountain Heroes

Wild Riders MC

Maple Springs

Men of Maple Mountain

All the Single Dads

Candy's Café

Small Town Sisters

For a full list of titles visit the Sadie King website

www.authorsadieking.com

ABOUT THE AUTHOR

Sadie King is a USA Today Best Selling Author of short instalove romance.

She lives in New Zealand with her ex-military husband and raucous young son.

When she's not writing she loves catching waves with her son, runs along the beach, and good wine, preferably drunk with a book in hand.

Keep in touch when you sign up for her newsletter. You'll even snag yourself a free short romance!

Visit: www.authorsadieking.com/free

www.authorsadieking.com

www.ingramcontent.com/pod-product-compliance
Lightning Source LLC
Chambersburg PA
CBHW021326160726
47994CB00004B/1639